# where's Leopold? ②

## Snowball Truce!

by Michel-Yves Schmitt
illustrated by Vincent Caut

Graphic Universe™ • Minneapolis • New York

The authors would like to thank Leopold's readers.

Thanks also to Vincent                    —Michel-Yves

Thanks also to Michel-Yves             —Vincent

Story by Michel-Yves Schmitt
Art by Vincent Caut
Translation by Carol Klio Burrell

English translation copyright © 2013 by Lerner Publishing Group, Inc.

First American edition published in 2013 by Graphic Universe™.
Published by arrangement with MEDIATOON LICENSING—France.

Où es-tu Léopold?
2/Un pacte en hiver
© DUPUIS 2011—Caut & Schmitt
www.dupuis.com

Graphic Universe™
A division of Lerner Publishing Group, Inc.
241 First Avenue North
Minneapolis, MN 55401 U.S.A.

Website address: www.lernerbooks.com

Library of Congress Cataloging-in-Publication Data

Schmitt, Michel-Yves.
     [Pacte en hiver. English]
     Snowball truce! / by Michel-Yves Schmitt ; illustrated by Vincent Caut ; translation by Carol
Klio Burrell. — 1st American ed.
          p.   cm. — (Where's Leopold? ; #2)
     Summary: Leopold wants to use his invisibility to launch the best snowball fight of all time, but
his older sister, Celine, thinks he should be using his powers for the greater good.
     ISBN 978-1-4677-0770-1 (lib. bdg. : alk. paper)
     ISBN 978-1-4677-1657-4 (eBook)
     1. Graphic novels. [1. Graphic novels. 2. Brothers and sisters—Fiction. 3. Invisibility—
Fiction.] I. Caut, Vincent, ill. II. Burrell, Carol Klio. III. Title.
PZ7.7.S37Sno 2013
741.5'944—dc23                                                              2012042495

Manufactured in the United States of America
1 – MG – 7/15/13

You have a superpower that you could save the world with!

But nooo, you just want to throw snowballs!

You could catch thieves...

TA-DA!

End wars...

?

?

TA-DA!

Sneak into the secret bases of master criminals...

TA-DA! GOTCHA!

I could do all that?

Yes, of course! If you wanted!

But to do that, you'd have to stop teasing your sister by turning invisible!

Deal?

SPLAT

I'd rather tease you!

Hee hee hee!

Your childish tricks are such a pain, Leo!

Why don't we make a truce?

You stop playing invisible pranks on me . . .

. . . and I promise that I won't take your slice of cake!

Let's shake on it!

See, there you go AGAIN!

I'm REALLY COLD!

AAAA...

CHOO

102° fever! Poor Celine...

OK, no school for three or four days.

Three or four days?

LUCKY!

I'm going outside...

...I'm gonna roll in the snow!

The Fantabulous Four are the best!

I wish I had the powers of STONEMAN!

If I were as strong as him, I could carry SUPER-HEAVY things!

I'd want to be STRETCHY MAN and tangle up bad guys!

If I had that power, I could *see* all the *boys* in the bathroom!

I could *see* **you** **three**, for example!

GROSS! You can't do that!

Anyway, that power doesn't really exist!

Are you sure?

Hee hee hee!

You better lock the bathroom door, just in case!

Kids, this is Melanie.

She's your babysitter tonight. Be good!

Hi, kids...Do you want to play a game?

YEAH!

HIDE-AND-SEEK!

Oh **NO**...

Why not?

With him, this game isn't much fun...

Go on. I'll count! Leopold, find a place to hide!

In this room is fine...

1, 2, 3...

This winter in our yard, Mr. Snowman sat.

He had two woolly gloves and a red pot for a hat.

He had a body like a marshmallow and a head like an ice-cream scoop.

THE END

**Michel-Yves Schmitt** was born in Bordeaux, France, but he grew up in the city of Nantes. He studied both applied arts and fine arts before moving to Paris to become a graphic designer. During these early years, he drew cartoons for the zines *Beurk!* and *Goinfre*. Later, his work appeared mostly in professional publications, including the comic magazine *Patate Douce*. Schmitt is the author and illustrator of the slice-of-life graphic novels *Dérives, Ainsi danse*, and *Ma vie d'adulte*. He also collaborated with artist Cédric Kernel to create a Wild West comic titled *La Poire en deux*. He then spent three years working as an artist on the Geronimo Stilton animated series. Most recently, he teamed up with Vincent Caut to create Où es-tu Léopold? (the French title for **Where's Leopold?** series), which received the Prize for School Comic at the Angoulême International Comics Festival in 2012.

Vincent Caut was born in Melun, a suburb of Paris. At the age of thirteen, he discovered webcomics and decided to make his own. Eight years later, he was awarded the Grand Prize for Promising Young Talent and the Revelation Second Prize at the Angoulême International Comics Festival. He then wrote and drew his first book, *Le Trésor de l'Île Mokoko*. His other solo works include *Quelle Tête en l'Air!*, *Les Aventures de la Fin du Monde*, and *Soit dit en passant, journal d'un étudiant*. He teamed up with Sophie Lamoureux to create a graphic novel about the Plains Indians called *Les Indiens d'Amérique à petits pas*. It was around this time that he collaborated with Michel-Yves Schmitt to create **Where's Leopold?**